Holly Horse
And the
Great Quest

"A beautifully illustrated children's story with animals, nature and valuable life lesson"

Written By Jenny Loveless

Illustrated by Nia Onit

Holly Horse
And the
Great Quest

Holly Horse had lots of things. She had plenty of room to run and play. She always had food and water in her trough, and endless fields of grass to snack on.

Holly felt happy most of the time. Sometimes though, she couldn't help but feel that there might be something more out there, just waiting for her to find.

One morning while Holly was snacking on some fresh grass, the little horse overheard something. She heard one of her sister's say, "the greenest, most delectable grass." That was enough for Holly. She had to know more.

6

Holly's sisters were just finishing munching on their own snack, when Holly darted toward them. Luckily, she caught them just in time.

"Wait, wait, where?" Holly asked. Her two sisters stopped and waited curiously.

"Where what?" one of them responded.

"The grass," Holly said. "Where can I find the greenest, most delectable grass?"

"Oh yeah, that, that's on the other side!"

But before Holly could find out more, her two sisters had already run off.

Holly Horse was so happy to hear about this. She had been right all along. There was something more out there. But she still had no idea where to look. She knew it was on the other side, but... the other side of what, she wondered. Holly had never been outside of her own ranch before. The only thing she had ever seen beyond it was the mountains, not too far in the distance. "That's it," Holly said to herself. "It must be on the other side of those mountains!"

And this is how the quest for the greenest, most delectable grass began.

10

Holly's journey to the foot of the mountains was very peaceful. With every breath she took, she could smell the beautiful flowers that filled the fields. Holly knew she would miss this while she was gone, but she was already on her way.

The curious horse slowed down when she saw a trail leading up the mountains. Holly only got a few feet onto the trail when she heard a voice call from behind her.

"You're not going to cross those mountains by yourself, are you?" Holly turned around to see a little white goat with a beard coming toward her.

"Yes, I have to get to the other side of these mountains!" she exclaimed.

"Oh no, you shouldn't go alone," the little goat said. "I'm Gary, Gary Goat. I go this way every day. I walk a bit slow, but you can come along with me if you would like. These mountains are much too dangerous to cross by yourself."

"I would love to," said Holly. "Thank you!" So the two new friends started up the trail.

While Holly Horse and Gary Goat climbed the trail together, Holly could see the light dimming in the sky. Holly always loved watching the sunset, but this one was different. "The sunset is pretty," she told the goat. "But not nearly as beautiful as they are back home. There, the sunset looks like a rainbow exploded into the sky like fireworks."

"I bet it's lovely," Gary said.

"Oh, It is." Holly wished she could see that tonight.

15

After a long trek over the mountains, the two finally found themselves on the other side. It was dark now. "Well, this is it," the goat informed her as they reached the bottom of the trail. Then Gary flashed Holly a smile and said, "Just keep moving kid, you'll find what you're looking for!" Holly thanked Gary, and then watched him in the moonlight as he continued on his way.

18

Holly Horse made it to the other side of the mountains, but when she got there, the grass didn't look any different than the grass found back at home. She felt a bit disappointed, but she knew the special grass was out there somewhere. Holly decided that if she wanted to find this delectable treat, she would have to keep going.

Holly walked until she noticed some very tall trees beginning to surround her. She had never seen trees this big before. Holly also noticed a big shiny brown bird sitting on a low branch. It had big bright yellow eyes. Holly had never seen a bird like this before either.

"Excuse me," she said.

"Hoo!"

"Who? I'm talking to you of course. There is no one else around."

The big creature swooped down and settled himself on a fallen tree log, closer to Holly.

"I'm an owl," he laughed, "'hoo' is what we say."

Holly Horse turned pink in the cheeks.

"And there are lots of others around, they're just hiding," the owl continued.

"Are they hiding from you?" asked Holly.

"Hoo, me? No, not me."

So Holly asked him, "Are they hiding from me?"

"Hoo, you? No, not you."

"Then who?" Holly asked, puzzled.

"And I thought I was the owl," the bird said.

The owl called Holly to him with a wave of his wing. Holly then, bent down low enough so they were face-to-face.

"They're hiding from the night," he whispered. "Many sleep at the end of the day, but many others come out to play!" Holly liked this owl. She thought he was silly.

"This isn't your neck of the woods my dear, you shouldn't be here!" the owl warned.

"But I'm already here and I've come so far!"

"You are here," he said, "Yes, you are, but if you're not careful you won't get far."

Holly's new friend thought for a moment. "Come on, I'll take you to the other side of the forest," he said. "I can see everything in the dark. There is no one better than me in this entire forest, who can get you there."

"Oh, thank you!" Holly exclaimed. "By the way, I'm Holly."

"Hello Holly, I'm Ollie." He said.

Both Holly and Ollie had a good laugh.

24

The forest was very dark. As she walked, Holly looked up at the sky again. This time, all she saw was one bright lonely star.

"Ollie, why do you only have one star in your sky?"

"They're hiding, dear," Ollie said. Holly looked closely through the darkness and saw all of the treetops that were blocking her view of the sky.

"Where I live, you can see a million stars," she told him. "It looks like a mountain of glitter was tossed into the sky." Holly wished she could see the stars tonight.

It was a relief for Holly to see the sun coming up. Ollie was relieved too. He had been flying all night leading Holly through the forest, now he could rest his wings.

"If you keep going straight, you will come to the edge of the woods in no time," Ollie said.

"Where are you going?" Holly asked him.

"Beauty sleep my dear, these good looks don't happen overnight you know!" Ollie gave Holly a wink, and then was gone. Holly Horse was alone again.

When Holly finally saw an opening in the brush, she whinnied with excitement. Once she made her way through the opening, she found herself at a quaint little pond. It was the perfect place to rest after her long journey. By this time, the sun was high in the sky.

Holly was very thirsty, and the pond water looked so refreshing. The morning sun added a dazzling layer of diamonds that skimmed the surface of the water. Holly took a large drink from it, only to end up with a thick string of slimy moss stuck in her teeth. She sucked the moss loose and spit it out. "Yuck!" she muttered.

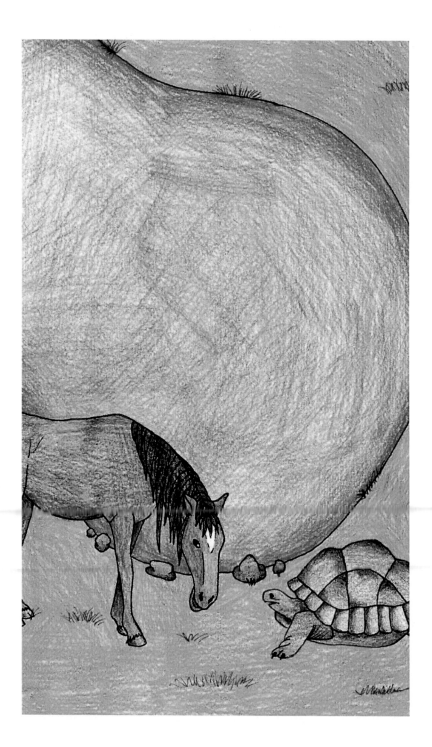

"What's the matter? Don't you like moss?" Holly looked over and discovered a very large tortoise basking in the sun.

"Good morning," said Holly.

"And good morning to you. I'm Mr. Tim Tortoise," the tortoise said to her.

"I'm Holly," she simply replied.

Holly turned to the water again longing to take another drink. But she really didn't want another mouthful of moss, so she decided against it.

"The water looks delicious, doesn't it?" said Mr. Tortoise.

"Yes it does," Holly agreed. "But it sure doesn't taste delicious."

"That's because things aren't always what they seem to be."

Holly hung her head and said, "No, I guess not." Holly was beginning to think this whole trip wasn't what it seemed to be. She still hadn't found the greenest, most delectable grass.

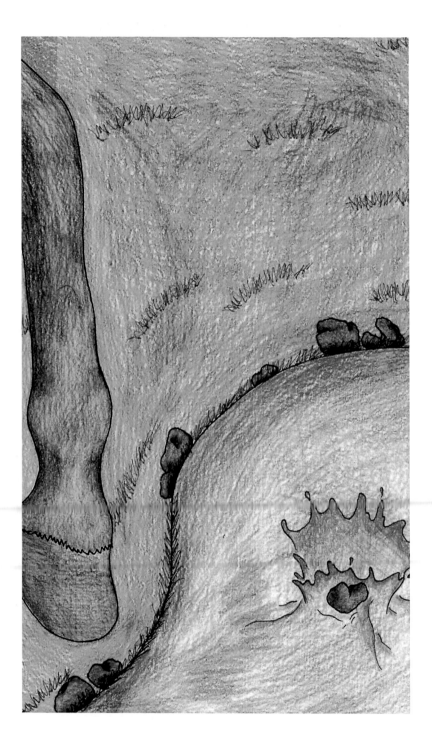

32

"Tell me your troubles, little one. Maybe I can help," Mr. Tortoise offered.

The discouraged horse kicked a rock into the pond and said, "Thank you. That's very kind of you, but you can't help me. No one can. I've looked everywhere."

"Oh, I love hide-and-go-seek," the large tortoise began. "It may take me a year to get somewhere, but I do know where everything is. I've lived here for 72 years." When Holly heard Mr. Tim Tortoise say this, her eyes sparkled. She jumped for joy and asked, "Mr. Tortoise, do you know where I can find the greenest, most delectable grass?"

"Like I said, I know where everything is," Mr. Tortoise told her, pointing his nose to a little stone bridge. When Holly Horse saw the bridge, she threw herself up onto her hind legs and took off, shouting "Thank you Mr. Tortoise!" Mr. Tortoise just closed his eyes, smiled, and went right back to basking in the sun.

36

Holly Horse was up and over that bridge faster than her feet had ever taken her before. And there it was, the greenest, most delectable grass! It was practically glowing. It was the most beautiful thing Holly's eyes had ever seen.......or so she thought.

But then Holly saw something absolutely amazing, something even better than the greenest, most delectable grass. Holly Horse saw a big wooden arch that read "Home Sweet Home Ranch." The reason this was so absolutely amazing was because her own ranch was called "Home Sweet Home Ranch."

Holly Horse was home!

38

Holly was right after all. The grass was greener on the other side, the other side of her very own ranch. Now there was only one thing to do. Holly smiled from ear to ear and took a great big bite.

From that day on, Holly Horse was thankful that she didn't have to go far to find what she was looking for. All she had to do was look in her own back yard.

The End

About the Author

 Jenny Loveless was born in Saint Louis Missouri in 1977. She now resides in California with her husband and her three beautiful daughters. After working in the childcare field for nearly 20 years, she is now a stay-at-home mom and an author of parenting books for you and inspirational children's books for your kids.

Jenny Loveless' dream of becoming an author has come true. Now one of her main goals in life is to help lift children to their fullest potential through her writings, so they too, will grow up and achieve their goals, and love and inspire others in the process.

Made in the USA
San Bernardino, CA
26 April 2016